Princess

Princess Ellie's Perfect Plan

Ellie was just closing Sundance's door when the sound of running feet made her swing round. It was Kate, and her face was streaked with tears.

"I won't go!" she sobbed. "I won't! I won't!"

Look out for more sparkly adventures of
The Pony-Mad Princess!

The Pony-Mad Princess

Princess Ellie's Perfect Plan

Diana Kimpton

Illustrated by Lizzie Finlay

USBORNE

GROOMING

First published in 2014 by Usborne Publishing Ltd.,
Usborne House, 83-85 Saffron Hill, London EC1N 8RT, England.
www.usborne.com

Based on an original concept by Anne Finnis.

A CIP catalogue record for this book is available from the British Library.

ISBN 9781409556787 JFMAM JASOND/14 02892/1

Printed in Chatham, Kent, UK.

Chapter 1

"Go on, boy," urged Princess Ellie, as she cantered Sundance across the palace paddock. The jumping lesson was nearly over. This was her last try at the course, and she was determined to go clear.

She headed Sundance towards the first fence. The chestnut pony responded willingly and cleared the two crossed poles with space to spare.

Ellie felt a surge of excitement – she loved jumping. But she knew she mustn't let her attention slip so she pushed away all her other thoughts and focused on the next fence: a single horizontal pole.

Sundance bounded over that just as easily and, as soon as they landed, Ellie turned him to the right and headed for the next jump. It was another single pole but this time the space underneath was filled with a piece of wood painted with bright red and yellow stripes.

Sundance snorted when he saw it, and Ellie felt him slow slightly and try to swing to the right. She pressed her legs against his sides to urge him onwards and managed to keep him going straight towards the fence.

Princess Ellie's Perfect Plan

Sundance snorted again when he reached it and jumped much higher than Ellie expected.

He flew over the pole and landed so hard that he almost jolted Ellie out of the saddle. But she kept her balance and turned him left towards the last fence.

It was a double jump: two cross-pole fences set very close together. As Sundance approached the first fence, Ellie concentrated on the vital space between that one and the next. Should she try to get Sundance to cover it in two strides and risk being too far away from the second half of the double or should she let him take three and risk being too close?

She made her decision as Sundance cleared the first fence. She lined him up to the second half and counted his strides, "One, two, three." Then Sundance took off and for a moment, she thought he'd cleared that fence too. But as he landed, he clipped one of the poles with a hind foot, and it fell to the ground.

"Bad luck," called her best friend, Kate,

who was sitting in the saddle of a grey pony. "That's exactly what Rainbow did with me."

"Never mind," said Meg, the palace groom, as she walked over to them. "You both did very well. Doubles are tricky. You just need a bit more practice with them."

"Could we try jumping against the clock next time?" asked Ellie. "It looks like fun when I watch riders do that on TV."

"It looks scary too," said Kate. "But I've got to learn to do it if I'm going to ride in the Olympics one day."

Meg laughed. "So that's your plan, is it?" She glanced at Ellie. "And what about you? Are you heading for international competition too?"

"I'd love to," said Ellie. Then she shook her head and sighed. "But Dad won't let me go in for any horse shows, even local ones. He says loads of reporters would turn up to take pictures of me and spoil the show for everyone else.

And the flashes on their cameras might frighten the ponies and cause an accident."

"I suppose he's got a point," said Meg. She gave Ellie a sympathetic smile and added, "Being a princess has some drawbacks."

"Maybe I should be glad I'm not royal," said Kate, whose grandmother was the palace cook. She reached forward and stroked the grey pony's neck. "But there are some good bits to being a princess. And Rainbow is definitely one of them."

"So is Sundance," Ellie agreed with a grin. "And Starlight and Moonbeam and Shadow." Having five ponies helped make up for the restrictions of being royal. And having Kate as her best friend made life even better.

The Pony-Mad Princess

"I think that's enough jumping for today," said Meg. "The ponies are getting tired." She turned and headed towards the stables, leaving Ellie and Kate to ride back together.

As they walked their ponies side by side, Kate looked at her watch. "Mum and Dad should be back by now. I'm dying to know where they've been today."

Princess Ellie's Perfect Plan

"Didn't they tell you?" asked Ellie.

Kate shook her head. "They were very secretive about it. But they said they might come back with some exciting news."

"Wow!" said Ellie. "Do you want to go straight home to find out what it is? I can untack Rainbow for you." She knew her friend wanted to spend as much time as she could with her parents while they were here. They worked abroad most of the time so she only saw them when they came back for their holidays.

"That would be great," said Kate. As soon as they reached the yard, she jumped down from Rainbow's back and handed her reins to Ellie. She ran to the end stable and stroked the nose of her own pony, Angel. Then she raced off towards the apartment at the back of the palace where she lived with her grandparents.

Ellie dismounted too and led the ponies towards their stables. She untacked them both and brushed the saddle marks from their backs. Then she fetched two bulging haynets that Meg had filled earlier and hung one up for each of them.

She was just closing Sundance's door when the sound of running feet made her swing round. It was Kate, and her face was streaked with tears.

"I won't go!" she sobbed. "I won't! I won't!"

Chapter 2

Kate raced across the yard and dived into Angel's stable. Ellie ran after her. Something awful must have happened. She'd never seen Kate so upset before.

When she stepped into the stable, she found Kate with her arms around her brown and white pony's neck and her face buried in her mane. That was silky soft now Angel was a yearling, and it no longer stood straight up like it had when she was a foal.

Ellie moved as close to Kate as she could get, hoping her presence would be comforting. "What's wrong?" she asked. "Where won't you go?"

"To boarding school," said Kate. "Mum and Dad want to send me to some horrible school that's miles and miles away from you and the stables and Angel."

Ellie stared at her in horror. "But you can't go. You're my best friend." She'd been so lonely before Kate came to live with her grandparents at the palace while her parents worked abroad.

"I know. I told them that. And I told them I'm happy at the school I'm at now. But they don't care."

"Yes, we do," said Kate's dad from the doorway. His voice made Ellie jump – she'd been concentrating so hard on Kate that she hadn't heard her friend's parents arrive.

Kate swung around, her face flushed with anger. "If you cared, you wouldn't be sending me away."

"It's for your own good," said her mum. She walked over and tried to put her arms around her daughter. But Kate pushed her off.

"Calm down, sweetie," said her dad, as he stepped towards her. "We just want you to have a good education."

"But I'm already getting one at the school in the village."

"Not for ever," said her dad, as he walked across the stable. He stroked Angel's face and added, "Your pony isn't the only one who is growing up. You'll have to change to a different school soon, and we've chosen the best possible one for you to go to."

"But I want to stay here with Angel and Ellie and Gran and Grandad."

"And I want Kate to stay too," said Ellie. "We're best friends."

"We know," said Kate's mum. "But we're not separating you for ever. You'll still be together in the holidays."

"But I'll be away for ages," wailed Kate. "I'll hate this school. I know I will."

Princess Ellie's Perfect Plan

Kate's dad patted her on the shoulder. "We're sure you'll change your mind when you see the place. That's why we're taking you to visit it tomorrow."

"Tomorrow!" said Kate. "But I'm supposed to be at my own school then."

"No problem," said her dad. "We've arranged for you to have the day off. Your teacher said she'd allow it as we're so rarely here."

"It will be lovely to spend the whole day together," said Kate's mum. "We can have a meal while we're out and do some shopping. You could get a new headcollar for Angel."

She paused as if she was waiting for her daughter to say something in response. But Kate stayed sullenly silent and huddled closer to her pony. Eventually her mum gave up waiting and turned to leave. "We'd best be getting back. I promised Gran we'd help with supper so please come in soon."

"What am I going to do?" said Kate, when her parents were safely out of earshot. She hugged Angel even tighter and started to cry again. "I don't want to go, but they've made up their minds."

"So we'll just have to unmake them," said Ellie. "There must be some other solution – one that doesn't involve you going away."

Princess Ellie's Perfect Plan

They fetched Angel's hay while they were thinking. Then they leaned over her stable door and watched her eat. "It's so unfair," said Kate. "It's my life, but Mum and Dad aren't listening to what I want."

"I wonder if your parents would listen to mine," said Ellie. "Surely they'd have to let you stay if the King and Queen told them to."

"That would be brilliant," said Kate, looking hopeful for the first time since she came back. "Can you get them to do it?"

"I don't know," said Ellie, trying not to give her friend false hope. "But I promise I'll try."

Angel tugged a mouthful of hay from the net and popped her head over the door while she ate it. Kate stroked her in her favourite spot, just behind her ears. Then she turned to Ellie. "If I do have to go, will you spend some time with Angel every day I'm away?"

"Of course I will," Ellie promised. But she

hoped desperately that she would never have to do it. Life at the palace would be so lonely without Kate.

Chapter 3

When Ellie got back to the palace, she swapped her riding clothes for a frothy pink dress, tugged a comb through her hair and put a tiara on her head instead of her everyday crown. Then she ran downstairs to join her parents for dinner with the Prime Minister.

She was only just in time. The adults

Princess Ellie's Perfect Plan

 were already there and, as soon as she'd sat down, the maids served everyone with prawn cocktails in glittering, crystal dishes. Usually the sight of them made Ellie's mouth water, but today she was too worried about Kate to care much about the food.

"Why the glum face, Aurelia?" asked the King as he finished his last mouthful. He always insisted on using her full name, although she would rather he didn't.

"Kate's parents want to send her to boarding school," said Ellie. "And I don't want her to go. She's my friend."

"I know," said the Queen with a sympathetic smile. "I'm sure you'll miss her, but I'm also sure that Kate's parents have her best interests at heart."

"Boarding schools can be fun," said the Prime Minister.

"Mine wasn't," said the King. "I hated it. There were too many cold showers and cross-country runs. We slept in horrid dormitories with not enough blankets, and the food was awful."

Ellie shuddered. "Did your parents know it was that bad?"

"My father did. He'd been there himself and said cold showers were character-forming."

Princess Ellie's Perfect Plan

The Queen laughed. "I'm glad I had a governess like you, Aurelia. Having lessons at the palace sounds a much safer option. I like my showers nice and warm."

So did Ellie. She shuddered at the idea of what lay ahead for Kate. It was bad enough thinking of her best friend going away. It was even worse to think of her going somewhere horrible. Ellie had to do something to stop it.

She was about to ask her parents for help, when the maids returned. They whisked away the empty dishes and replaced them with generous portions of succulent roast beef and piping-hot roast vegetables.

By then, the adults had started talking about other topics. Ellie wasn't remotely interested in banking, taxes or elections so she concentrated on her food, while she waited for a gap in the conversation so she could ask them to help Kate.

The pudding was a delicious baked Alaska. Ellie couldn't work out how Kate's gran managed to cook the meringue on the outside without melting the ice cream inside. But, however she did it, the result was delicious.

"You still look sad," said the Prime Minister, when Higginbottom, the butler, had finished pouring peppermint tea into their gold-rimmed cups. "I know just the thing to cheer you up."

He pulled a pack of cards from his pocket and gave them a quick shuffle. Then he spread them into a fan shape and offered them to her. "Take a card, but don't let me see what it is."

Ellie was tempted to let him have an accidental peep. He was so bad at magic that he needed all the help he could get. But she was sure he'd be disappointed if she did, so she hid the Five of Clubs behind her hands while she looked at it. Then she kept it face down when she pushed it back into the pack.

The King and Queen stopped talking to watch the trick. The sudden silence gave Ellie the chance she'd been waiting for. "Can you talk to Kate's parents about the boarding school?" she asked.

A flicker of suspicion showed in the King's eyes. "Are you up to something, Aurelia?" he asked.

Ellie felt her face flush. But before she had time to say anything, the Prime Minister pulled a card from the pack and waved it at her. "Did you pick the Queen of Hearts?" he asked.

"No," Ellie told him, as gently as she could.

The Prime Minister looked disappointed. Then he started to shuffle the cards again.

"You haven't answered my question," said the King.

Ellie looked him straight in the eye and summoned all her courage. "I just thought that if you told Kate's parents not to send her to school, they'd have to do what you said because you're the King and Queen."

The King and Queen stared at her. Their expressions made their disapproval clear.

"Was it the Four of Clubs?" asked the Prime Minister, apparently unaware of what was happening.

"Nearly," said Ellie, trying to be encouraging. Then she turned back to her parents and said, "It's so simple. You know you could do it."

"But we won't," said the Queen.

"It wouldn't be right for us to do it," said the King.

Ellie looked pleadingly at the Prime Minister. "Please tell them they're wrong." He'd helped to change her parents' minds before when she wanted to look after her ponies herself and when she wanted to go camping. Surely he would help her again now.

But he didn't. "Your parents are absolutely right. It would be a total misuse of royal power to order Kate's parents not to send her to school." Then he held the Five of Clubs out to Ellie and raised his eyebrows questioningly.

Princess Ellie's Perfect Plan

Ellie gave the briefest of nods in response. She was so upset about none of them helping her that she didn't care about the trick any more. But she still cared about Kate. Surely there was something else she could do to stop her going away?

Chapter 4

Next morning, Ellie felt lonely as soon as she awoke. It didn't usually worry her if Kate went out for the day, but today was different. Today she knew this is what it would be like all the time if Kate went to boarding school. There would be no meeting up at the stables before Kate caught the bus to the village school and no riding together after

Princess Ellie's Perfect Plan

Ellie's lessons had finished. Without Kate, Ellie would be alone all the time, just like she was before her best friend arrived.

She walked slowly to the palace schoolroom, still trying to think of a plan to stop Kate going away. When she arrived, her governess, Miss Stringle, was already there. "We'll start with English," she said, as she waited for Ellie to sit down at her desk.

Ellie sighed. English should have been her favourite subject. She loved reading, and the shelves in her bedroom were packed with pony books. But Miss Stringle always chose books for her to study that contained no horses at all.

The current one was about boats, and Ellie couldn't think of anything more boring. Worse still, she wasn't allowed just to read it. She had to write essays about it and do silly comprehension exercises that were even less interesting than the story.

"Please pay attention, Princess Aurelia," said Miss Stringle, halfway through the lesson. "Staring out of the window and daydreaming is not helping you learn."

Ellie sighed. That was the problem with having lessons by herself. Miss Stringle always noticed what she was doing, whether it was good or bad.

Suddenly Ellie had an idea. Suppose Kate could share Ellie's lessons with Miss Stringle?

Then she wouldn't have to go away to school, and they could be together all the time. Kate's dad couldn't possibly argue against that. If Miss Stringle's lessons were good enough for a princess, they must be good enough for Kate too.

Ellie smiled with satisfaction. It was the perfect solution. She just needed to get Miss Stringle and her parents to agree to it. The King and Queen had gone to the city for the day to open a museum and hand out degree certificates at the university. So she decided to tackle Miss Stringle first.

But she didn't ask her straight away. It seemed more sensible to make sure her governess was in a good mood first. So Ellie pushed away all thoughts of Kate and the ponies and concentrated hard on her work.

She sailed through the rest of the English lesson, got full marks in maths and remembered her best table manners during lunch.

By the time the last lesson of the day began, Miss Stringle was beaming with satisfaction. "We'll do history in the library," she announced. "My favourite subject in my favourite place."

Ellie was sure she would never get Miss Stringle in a better mood than this. For a few minutes, she settled down to her work with pretended enthusiasm. Then she plucked up her courage and raised her hand.

"Is there a problem, Princess Aurelia?" asked Miss Stringle.

"I was just thinking that I might learn better if I had someone to work with.

Someone the same age as me. Someone like Kate."

Miss Stringle was so shocked that she nearly dropped the book she was holding. "That's impossible. Kate's not royal."

"But she is my friend. And if she can't have lessons with me, she'll have to go away to boarding school."

Miss Stringle gave Ellie's hand a sympathetic pat. "I understand why that is upsetting. But we can't go against tradition. I am the Royal Governess, and the Royal Governess only teaches royal children."

Ellie opened her mouth to argue and then decided against it. There was no point. Tradition was one of the other drawbacks of being a princess. If that was on Miss Stringle's side, there was nothing Ellie could say that would make her change her mind.

Chapter 5

Ellie lost interest in her history books after
tradition and Miss Stringle killed her plan.
It was much more important to think of
another way for Kate to stay at the palace.
Ellie was determined to have some good
news to make her friend feel better when
she came back from visiting the horrid
boarding school.

It was a relief when lessons were finally over. Ellie ran up the spiral staircase to her bedroom and changed into her pink riding clothes. Then she put on a pale purple fleece that Kate had given to her. Maybe wearing that would make her feel closer to her friend.

The yard seemed very quiet when she arrived. It felt strange knowing Kate wouldn't join her at any minute. But she wasn't completely alone. Her ponies were still there. "You'll all have to be my friends instead," she said as she walked along the line of stables, stroking each of them in turn. "Now which of you shall I ride today?"

Shadow the Shetland whinnied in response, which made Ellie laugh. "Not you," she said, as she leaned over the door

and ran her fingers
through his black
mane. "You're
much too small
for me now."

She
straightened
up and looked
thoughtfully at
the others. She
and Kate had ridden
Sundance and Rainbow yesterday. Angel was
too young to be ridden and she belonged
to Kate anyway. So today it would be fair to
take Moonbeam, the palomino, or Starlight,
who was Angel's mother. Then she
remembered Moonbeam had a loose shoe
and that made the decision easy.

She fetched a headcollar and led Starlight into the sunshine. She tied the bay mare to a ring in the wall, fetched her grooming kit and set to work with the brushes. Normally she talked to Kate while she was at the yard, but today she talked to the pony instead. She told her everything about the Prime Minister's magic trick, Miss Stringle's boring English lesson and the awful possibility of Kate going away to school.

Starlight flicked her ears and listened. But she couldn't talk back. "It's not the same as having Kate here," sighed Ellie, as she stepped back to admire her handiwork. Starlight's brown coat gleamed in the sunshine. Her black mane and tail hung straight, smooth and tangle-free and so did the long hairs that covered her hooves.

Princess Ellie's Perfect Plan

"She looks good," said Meg, as she carried a bucket of water across the yard. "Are you going out for a ride?"

Ellie nodded. "I hoped you might come too." Having company would make her miss Kate less.

Meg shook her head. "I'm sorry. I've got to stay here. The farrier's coming soon to put new shoes on Moonbeam."

Ellie tried not to look too disappointed. If she couldn't think of a way to stop Kate going away, she would have to get used to being on her own. Maybe riding by herself wouldn't be as lonely as she feared.

She fetched Starlight's saddle and lifted it onto the pony's broad back. She was careful to put it too far forward so it smoothed the hairs underneath as she slid it back into place. Then she gently fastened the girth and ran her hand between the strap and Starlight's chest to make sure it wasn't pinching her.

Starlight looked pleased to be going out. She opened her mouth for the bit and lowered her head to make it easy for Ellie to slip the bridle over her ears and fasten the noseband and throatlatch. Then she stood perfectly still while Ellie tightened the girth, put her left foot in the stirrup and swung herself into the saddle.

Ellie was just sorting out her reins when Meg came over, holding a piece of paper. "It's a message from the farm manager," she explained. "He says we shouldn't go in Blunkett's Field this afternoon."

Princess Ellie's Perfect Plan

"Why not?" asked Ellie. Nothing was going right today. That field was one of her favourite places to ride.

"He doesn't say," said Meg. "But usually, when he tells us to stay out of a field, it's because they're using machinery that might frighten the ponies."

Ellie sighed. This felt like the last straw. First there'd been Kate's disastrous news, then both her plans to save her friend had failed and now she couldn't even ride wherever she wanted. If only Kate was with her. The day wouldn't feel so bad if they were together.

Chapter 6

Ellie cheered up a little as she rode Starlight out of the yard. It was a lovely sunny afternoon and, although Starlight couldn't chatter and laugh like Kate, she was still good company. The bay mare walked forward eagerly with her ears pricked, obviously enjoying being out for a hack.

As they passed the paddock, Ellie noticed

the jumping course was still in the same place it had been the day before. It reminded her of the fun she and Kate had had there yesterday. Neither of them had suspected then that their lives were about to change so much.

That memory made her more determined than ever to find a way to make sure Kate stayed at the palace. And she didn't want that just for her own sake. She hated the idea of Kate having to leave Angel behind and suffer the cold showers and bad food the King had described.

When they reached the deer park, she paused for a moment to plan a route for her ride that avoided Blunkett's Field. Then she cantered Starlight across the short, springy grass to the edge of the wood and turned onto a path that led between the trees. There were small jumps here made from piles of branches that she and Kate had pulled into position one Saturday.

Starlight pricked her ears forward and leaped over them with enthusiasm. She enjoyed jumping so much that Ellie took her over them several times, pretending they were in a competition. After a jump-off against her imaginary opponents, she won an equally imaginary red rosette and rode on, deeper and deeper into the wood.

The game had helped take her mind off the boarding school issue for a while. But now it was over, she started worrying about Kate again. She was so determined to find a solution to the problem that she barely paid any attention to where she was going.

Princess Ellie's Perfect Plan

She just ambled along on Starlight, following the path as it twisted and turned in the quiet shade of the spreading branches. And, when she came to the fork in the middle of the wood, she went left like she usually did when she was out with Kate, instead of right like she should have done today.

She only realized her mistake when she rode out of the darkness of the wood into the dazzling sunlight. She'd expected to be back at the deer park by now, but she wasn't. Instead she was at the top of a sloping field, neatly planted with rows of cabbages.

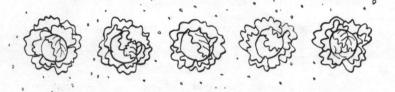

"Oh, no!" groaned Ellie. She'd gone completely wrong, and there were only two ways home from here. The quickest was the forbidden route through Blunkett's Field. The other involved going back the way she had come. But that would take ages, and there wasn't time. She'd already been out for nearly two hours, and the sun was low in the sky.

Princess Ellie's Perfect Plan

Ellie bit her lip thoughtfully. Perhaps she wouldn't feel so bad about going back if she understood why she couldn't go the short way. Ellie peered over the hedge into Blunkett's Field, searching for the reason. But all she saw was an awful lot of grass and one solitary cow standing all alone in the distance. Ellie felt sorry for it – it must feel as lonely as she did.

There was no farm machinery, scary or otherwise, and no people at all. They must have finished their work and gone home for the day. Surely, in that case, it must be safe for her to ride there, despite what the farm manager had said. And it would be stupid to make herself late home when there was no danger to avoid.

She rode Starlight down the field of

cabbages, being careful to keep to the edge so the pony's hooves didn't damage the crops. When she reached the gate to Blunkett's Field, she checked again that no one was around. Then she grabbed the latch, swung the gate open and rode Starlight inside.

She let the gate swing closed behind her and double-checked that it was fastened securely. Then she turned Starlight uphill and set off towards the top of the field.

The cow stopped grazing and looked at them. Ellie was closer to it now than she had been when she looked over the hedge, and she realized for the first time just how large it was. It had huge horns on its massive head and its chest was wide and powerful.

Princess Ellie's Perfect Plan

A tingle of apprehension ran down Ellie's back as the animal took a step towards them. "I've never seen a cow that big before," she told Starlight. "I hope it's friendly."

As if in answer, the creature pawed the ground with its front feet and bellowed with rage. That's when Ellie realized it wasn't a cow at all. It was a bull, and it was not pleased to have visitors.

Chapter 7

The bull bellowed again and pawed the ground harder. The sight of it made Ellie's stomach knot with nerves. The creature was working itself into a frenzy, ready to charge and trample them. If only she'd done as she was told and stayed out of Blunkett's Field. But there was no time for regrets now. She was in too much danger.

Princess Ellie's Perfect Plan

Starlight was frightened too. She danced on the spot and tugged at the reins, eager to get away. Ellie held her back. There was no point in running blindly. She had to work out the best way to escape.

The gate they had come through was the closest. But it was also close to the bull. Although Starlight would reach it first, they'd never get through it before the huge animal caught them up.

The other gate was away in the distance, at the top of the field. If they headed for that, they would be going uphill and the bull's enormous weight might slow it down enough for Starlight to race ahead. And if they were well in front when they reached the gate, they might have time to get through it before the bull caught up with them.

Ellie knew there were an awful lot of ifs in that plan, but it was the only one she could think of that would give them any chance at all. So she spun Starlight round so she was facing up the hill and squeezed her legs against the pony's sides.

She was just in time. As the bay mare leaped into a frenzied gallop, the bull finally charged in pursuit. The sound of their thundering hooves pounded in Ellie's ears as she leaned forward, balancing her weight on the stirrups like a jockey while Starlight ran to save both their lives.

The bull was massive, but he was fit and he was fast. He matched Starlight's speed as they raced across the grass. The bay mare stretched her neck forward and lengthened her stride, her mane and tail streaming behind

her in the wind. Ellie had never
galloped so fast in her life,
but she was far too
scared to enjoy it.

The gate at the top of the field came
closer and closer. Ellie glanced over her
shoulder, hoping to see that the bull was
slowing down. But he wasn't. He was just as
close as before, and he looked just as angry.

There was no way Ellie could get the
gate open before the bull caught them.
They were trapped in the field, unable
to do anything except run. And Starlight
was already breathing hard and starting
to tire. If she slowed down, the bull would
catch them.

Ellie shuddered at the thought of those
sharp horns and trampling hooves. Then she
realized there was still one way out of the
field. It was riskier than anything she had
ever done before, but it wasn't as dangerous
as staying where they were.

As they reached the top of the field, Ellie
used her seat and hands to steady Starlight's
mad rush and help her balance. Then she
pointed the bay mare at the gate and urged
her on.

Princess Ellie's Perfect Plan

Starlight realized immediately what Ellie wanted. She pushed off hard with her hind legs and soared into the air with her front feet tucked close to her body. It was a huge, brave jump that took them over the gate with centimetres to spare.

The Pony-Mad Princess

Ellie breathed a sigh of relief as the pony stretched out her front legs, ready to land. They were safe from the bull now. But, as Starlight's hooves touched the ground, she stumbled and pitched sideways. The sudden movement threw Ellie off balance, and her left foot slid out of the stirrup.

Starlight managed to regain her footing just in time, but Ellie didn't. She lost contact with the saddle, hurtled over the pony's shoulder and crashed to the ground.

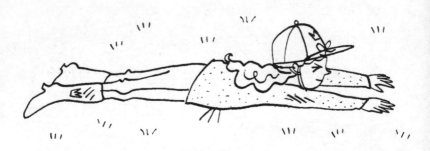

Chapter 8

Ellie lay still for a moment, too shocked by the fall to move. Everything seemed so calm and quiet now the desperate race was over and the sound of galloping hooves had gone. Then she sat up, anxious to find out if Starlight was all right.

She was relieved to spot the bay mare a couple of metres away. Starlight seemed uninjured, but her neck was damp with sweat and the rapid movement of her sides showed that she was breathing fast. She glanced fleetingly at Ellie. Then she looked over Ellie's head, flared her nostrils and stepped back fearfully.

Ellie turned to see what was worrying the pony and was shocked to find herself almost face-to-face with the bull. Although it was safely on the other side of the gate, it was menacingly close and still angry.

The bull bellowed again and rattled the gate with its horns. The sound made Starlight squeal in terror.

"Steady, girl," called Ellie. But the pony was too scared to listen. She whirled on the spot and galloped off at full speed.

Ellie watched in dismay as the bay mare disappeared into the distance. She couldn't be cross with her – Starlight was only acting on instinct, and she had saved them both with her fantastic jump. But now the pony had gone, Ellie had no alternative. She had to walk home.

She struggled to her feet, relieved to find that she was relatively unhurt. Although it had been a bad fall, the ground was soft so her only injuries were a few scratches and a bruise or two. She'd probably be stiff

tomorrow, but today she didn't feel
too bad.

She was sure Starlight would head
straight for the safety of the stables, so
she set off in the same direction. Every
time she rounded a bend in the path,
she hoped she'd find the pony grazing on
the other side so she could ride the rest of
the way. But she never did, so she had to
keep walking.

It was lonely out in the palace grounds
by herself and, for the umpteenth time that
day, she wished that Kate was with her.
None of this would have happened if she
hadn't been riding alone. She wouldn't
have taken the wrong path in the wood,
she wouldn't have been chased by the bull
and she wouldn't have fallen off.

Princess Ellie's Perfect Plan

Travelling on foot was much slower than going by horse, and Ellie wasn't used to walking so far. Before she was halfway home, she was tired and her feet ached. As she trudged wearily on, she wondered what had happened when Starlight arrived back without a rider. She was sure everyone would be worried about her. They might even send out search parties, but none of them would know where to look.

She had just reached the deer park when she spotted the royal Range Rover driving across the grass. "I'm over here," she yelled, as she ran towards it waving her arms.

The car veered in her direction. As it came closer, she saw Higginbottom behind the wheel and her parents in the back, crowded together so they could both wave at her through the nearest window.

As soon as the car stopped, the Queen jumped out and threw her arms around Ellie. "Thank goodness you're all right. We were worried you'd been hurt."

"Is Starlight okay?" Ellie asked when the hug was over.

"She's fine," said the King, who had followed closely behind his wife. "Meg's looking after her. But what happened? I'm guessing you didn't intend her to go home by herself."

"I fell," said Ellie. "But it wasn't her fault. She was brilliant. She saved us from the bull."

"The bull!" shrieked the Queen. "What bull?"

Ellie hesitated, wondering if there was some way she could avoid getting into trouble. But there was no way out – she had to tell the truth. "The bull in Blunkett's Field," she admitted quietly.

"Aurelia!" roared the King. "How dare you go in there when Meg had specifically told you not to?"

"I'm sorry – I really am," said Ellie. "But I got lost and it was late and that was the quickest way home."

"Even though there was a bull in the way," the King said sternly.

"It looked like a cow from a distance," said Ellie. She hated it when her dad was this cross.

The Queen patted her husband on the arm. "Calm down, dear. I'm sure Aurelia has learned an important lesson today about following rules."

"I have. I promise," said Ellie.

"I hope so," said the King, raising his eyebrows questioningly. "And I suppose falling off and having to walk home is enough punishment for today."

"I agree," said the Queen. "Now let's go home."

Ellie breathed a sigh of relief and clambered into the back seat between her parents. She knew she'd have to be on her best behaviour for a while, but that didn't stop her insisting that Higginbottom drove them straight to the stables. She wanted to check for herself that Starlight was safe and well.

"I'm still worried by how close you came to being hurt," said the Queen, as the car drove into the yard. "We must make sure that nothing like this ever happens again,"

Suddenly Ellie's hopes rose. Perhaps there was a way she could use the incident with the bull to help her best friend. "It's much safer riding out with someone else," she explained. "None of this would have happened if Kate had been with me."

Then she held her breath, wondering if her parents would take the hint.

Chapter 9

"I suppose you are safer riding with Kate," said the Queen, as they climbed out of the car.

Ellie grinned as they walked over to Starlight's stable. That was just what she'd hoped her mum would think. Now she just had to push a little harder. She stroked the bay mare's face and said, "If Kate goes to boarding school, I won't be able to ride with her any more. I'll have to ride on my own all the time."

"No you won't," said the King. "You can ride with Meg."

"But she's often too busy, and it's more fun with Kate."

There was a long pause, broken only by Starlight's gentle whicker as she nuzzled Ellie's pockets in search of treats. The dangers of the ride obviously hadn't dulled her appetite.

Princess Ellie's Perfect Plan

Eventually the King put a hand on Ellie's shoulder. "I know what you want us to do, Aurelia. But we've already told you that we can't. However much you want Kate to stay, it would still be wrong for us to order her parents not to send her to boarding school."

"That's a decision they have to make for themselves," said the Queen.

Ellie sighed. She'd tried everything she could think of, and there didn't seem to be any way to help Kate. But she could still make sure Starlight was all right. Although she knew Meg would have done that already, she wanted to be absolutely sure. So she buckled on the pony's headcollar, led her into the yard and tied her to a ring in the wall. Then she ran her hands down each of the pony's legs in turn, feeling for injuries.

"I'm surprised at you, Aurelia," said the King, as he watched Ellie work. "Usually you come up with lots of plots and plans to get your own way. But this time you've only had the one idea."

Princess Ellie's Perfect Plan

Ellie finished what she was doing and straightened up. "I did think of one other idea," she said. "But it won't work."

"Maybe we should be the judge of that," said the Queen. "What was it?"

"I thought Kate could share my lessons. Her dad would be sure to think that was a good enough education."

"I'm sure he would," the King agreed.

"And it would be fun for you too," said the Queen. "I would have loved a friend to share the lessons I had with my governess."

Ellie stared at them in surprise. She hadn't expected them to like her idea. "But Miss Stringle said it was impossible because Kate's not royal. She says that tradition decrees that the Royal Governess only teaches royal children."

The King nodded. "That's very true. Which is a pity because it was an excellent idea."

"It's so good that I'm not going to allow it to go to waste," declared the Queen in her firmest voice. "Tradition isn't fixed in stone. It's just what's always happened, and there are times when it needs to change."

"Like now?" asked Ellie.

"Definitely," said the King.

Ellie bounced up and down with excitement. "Do you mean Kate really can stay here and share my lessons."

"Provided her parents agree," said the King. "And I expect they will."

Ellie threw her arms around Starlight's neck and hugged her. "Did you hear that?" she said. "Everything's going to be all right."

Princess Ellie's Perfect Plan

At that moment, Kate ran into the yard, waving a brand-new headcollar for Angel in one hand and a rolled-up magazine in the other. "I'm back," she called.

"I've got some brilliant news," said Ellie, before her friend had a chance to say anything else.

"So have I," said Kate. "But you can tell me yours first."

"Mum and Dad say you can share my lessons with Miss Stringle. So you don't have to go away after all. You can stay here at the palace with Angel and me."

"But I don't want to," said Kate. "That's my exciting news. I've changed my mind. I want to go to boarding school."

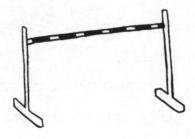

Chapter 10

Ellie stared at Kate in horror. "But you said you hated the idea."

"I know," said Kate. "But that was before I saw the school. Mum and Dad are right. It's absolutely perfect."

"It can't be," said Ellie. "What about the cold showers?"

Kate opened her eyes wide with

astonishment. "What are you talking about?"

"Dad's told me all about boarding school. When he went, he had to have a cold shower every morning. The food was awful and the dormitories were horrid."

"It was dreadful," the King agreed. "I hated every minute."

"But this one's not like that," said Kate. "There are pretty bedrooms instead of dormitories, there was plenty of hot water when I washed my hands and the food is lovely. We had a delicious lunch. And there—"

Princess Ellie's Perfect Plan

"But what about Angel?" Ellie interrupted. "Surely you don't want to leave her?"

Kate grinned. "I don't have to. I can take her with me. The school is specially designed for horse lovers. It's got its own riding school and stables, a cross-country course, a dressage arena and loads of showjumps. They even have their own horse shows for the pupils to enter, and two of the past students have gone on to ride in the Olympics."

"Oh!" said Ellie. It sounded so fantastic that it would be almost impossible to change her friend's mind now.

Kate was bouncing with enthusiasm. "They have riding lessons in the timetable so you end up with riding qualifications as well as non-horsey ones. When I'm not practising for the Olympics, I'd like to be a vet or a riding instructor."

Ellie swallowed hard and blinked back the tears that had filled her eyes. Kate was so excited that she seemed to have forgotten they were friends. "What about me?" she said quietly. "I'll be left here all on my own."

"No, you won't," said Kate. "You can come with me. I've already asked, and they've got a place for you if you want it."

Ellie stepped back in shock, her mouth

dry with fear at the thought of such a big change. She'd never been to school before, and she'd never lived away from home. "I'm not sure I want to do that," she admitted eventually. "It's too scary."

"But it's a wonderful place," said Kate. She unrolled the magazine she was carrying and pushed it into Ellie's hands. "Look at the brochure and you can see for yourself."

Ellie opened it and started to read, hoping to find something that would give her an excuse not to go – something that might make Kate stay at the palace too. But, as she turned the pages, she gradually discovered why her friend was so excited. The brochure was packed with pictures of young people studying and riding and generally enjoying themselves. The stables looked beautiful, and  so did the surrounding countryside.

"It looks much nicer than my old school," said the King, who was looking over Ellie's shoulder.

Princess Ellie's Perfect Plan

"The children look so happy," added the Queen.

But it wasn't just the photos that were tempting. The descriptions of the school were as well. Sport with Miss Stringle was limited to country walks, sedate games of croquet and an occasional dip in the palace swimming pool. There was much more on offer at the school – as well as all sorts of riding, there were team games like football, hockey and basketball that were impossible for Ellie to play on her own.

Even the lessons sounded as if they might be interesting. There were proper labs for science, a huge art studio and a workshop where pupils could make things out of wood and metal. Ellie liked the idea of doing that. It would make a welcome change from genteel embroidery with Miss Stringle and so would making her own bridle during saddlery lessons.

The last picture in the brochure showed a group of

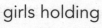

girls holding

rosettes and silver cups they had won in school horse shows. Ellie stared at them enviously. She wanted to be like them and enter competitions on her ponies. But that would never happen if she stayed at the palace.

Ellie looked up and grinned at Kate. "It looks brilliant."

"It is," said Kate. "So say you'll come. Please. It will be much more fun if you're there too."

Princess Ellie's Perfect Plan

Ellie's eyes shone with excitement. Deep inside, she still felt very slightly scared, but the chance of going to a horsey boarding school with Kate was too fantastic to turn down. There was just one problem – the decision wasn't just hers to make.

She turned to her parents and grinned. "Can I go? Please? I really want to."

To her dismay, the King shook his head sadly. "I'm sorry, Aurelia. That's not possible."

"Princesses in this country do not go to school," said the Queen. "Tradition decrees that they all have governesses."

Ellie slumped with disappointment, her dreams of school disappearing as fast as they had appeared. Then Starlight nudged her hard with her nose, as if she was telling her not to give up yet.

That's when Ellie remembered the conversation they'd had just before Kate came home. "You said tradition is what used to happen, and sometimes it can change. Maybe I can start a new tradition by being the first princess to go to school."

The King and Queen put their heads close together and had a whispered conversation. Then they turned back to Ellie and smiled. "It sounds as if you've found the perfect plan," said the King. "So we'll let you go."

"Provided that's what you really want," said the Queen.

"It is. It is!" shrieked Ellie. She threw one arm around Kate and the other around Starlight's neck and pulled the three of them together for a group hug. "We're going to

Princess Ellie's Perfect Plan

have huge fun at boarding school." This
was going to be her biggest adventure yet
and best of all, she and Kate were going to
stay together.

Pony-Mad Fun & Facts

Dear Reader,

Are you as pony-mad as Princess Ellie?
I am. I've loved ponies for as long as I can
remember. But I didn't get the pony I
dreamed of until I was grown up.

When I was a child, I had to make do
with reading about ponies and making up
imaginary stories about them. Maybe
that's why I write pony books now.

I hope you enjoy Princess Ellie's
adventures and, because I remember how
much I loved learning about ponies, there
are some fantastic facts and fun quiz
questions just for you in the following
pages...

Love,

Diana
xx

Factfile

Olympic Riding Events

If Kate's dream of riding in the Olympics came true, there are several different events she could enter...

SHOW JUMPING Competitors jump a course of fences with penalties for knocking down fences, refusing to jump and for exceeding the time limit.

DRESSAGE Sometimes called ballet for horses, this takes place in an arena with a soft surface and special markers. The horse and rider have to ride a set series of movements around the arena, changing pace and direction in exactly the right place.

EVENTING This takes place in three stages. In the first stage, the competitors complete a dressage test. The next day, they ride a cross country course with fences that are fixed so they don't fall down if the horse hits them. There are penalties for refusals and for exceeding the time limit, but a fall means automatic elimination. On the final day, the competitors ride a show jumping course.

Medals are awarded for the best individual horses and for the best team.

Princess Ellie's Pony-Mad Quiz

Do you know your **stirrup** from your **saddle**? Or who Ellie's **best friend** is? Test your knowledge of Princess Ellie's world with this quiz!

1. What type of animal is kept in Blunkett's Field?

a) A cow
b) A bull
c) A goat

2. The Royal Governess is called:

a) Miss Dingle
b) Miss Fingle
c) Miss Stringle

3. A person who rides a horse in a race is called:

a) A jockey
b) A pilot
c) A driver

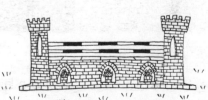

4. In show jumping, a double is:
a) A fence with two poles
b) A fence with two planks
c) Two fences close together that count as one

5. As well as competing in the Olympics and being a riding instructor, Kate wants to be:
a) A vet
b) A train driver
c) A policewoman

6. Snaffle, pelham and kimblewick are all types of:
a) Stirrup
b) Pony
c) Bit

The answers

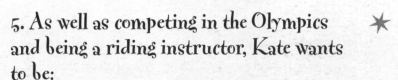

Tot up your total to see just how pony-mad you are...

1-3 A good try.

4-5 Great knowledge and a big rosette!

6 You are totally pony-mad – it's a **gold cup** for you!

Did you know...?
All about shoes and shoeing

Princess Ellie knows how important it is to take good care of ponies' feet, otherwise they may go lame. Here are her fantastic facts...

* Not all ponies wear shoes. If they don't, they are said to be "barefoot".

* Hooves grow all the time, like toenails, so ponies need their feet trimmed every six to eight weeks.

* The person who puts shoes on horses is called a farrier. The farrier takes off the old shoes, trims the feet and puts on new shoes.

* The shoes are held on with nails through the wall of the hoof. This doesn't hurt the pony because the wall is like a very thick fingernail.

* Most horseshoes are made of iron so they are heavy. Racehorses wear special lightweight shoes made of aluminium, called "racing plates".